Once a boy won a race!

by

Phoebe Beckett-McInroy and Isabel Looby

*"This book is dedicated to everyone in the world.
We hope you all succeed and score the goals you want to achieve."*

Phoebe and Isabel

Once a Boy Won a Race by Pheobe Beckett-McInroy and Isabel Looby

Printed 2016

ISBN 978-0-9931999-2-9

Published in the UK by Beckett McInroy Publishing

Beckett McInroy Consultancy SPC CR: 79249 © 2015

ONCE A BOY WON A RACE!

A boy runs and wants to come first in a race.
Find out how he wins when you read this book.

There was a boy who loved running races and sprints.

But unfortunately, he never won.

Then he trained SO HARD that every 5 minutes

he had to stop and wipe his sweat!

He kept training, and training, and training!

Then he signed up for a race and guess what?

He came third!

Then he goes to the supermarket to get lots of

energy drinks, fruit and vegetables.

Then he goes training again!!!

He keeps thinking about coming 1st.

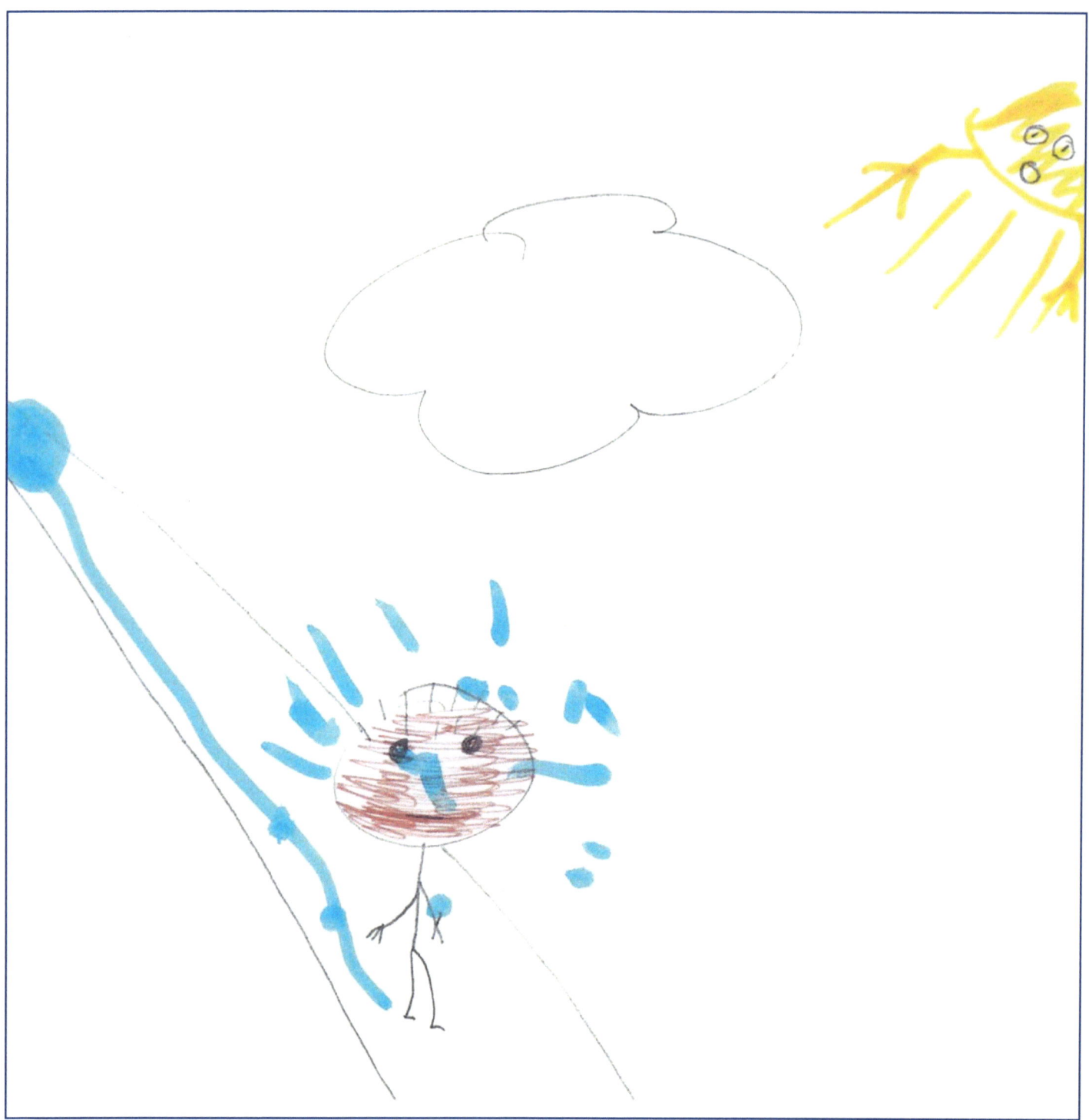

Eventually he enters another race and he comes…

St.

3 st   1 st   2 st

First !

Then he has a PARTY!

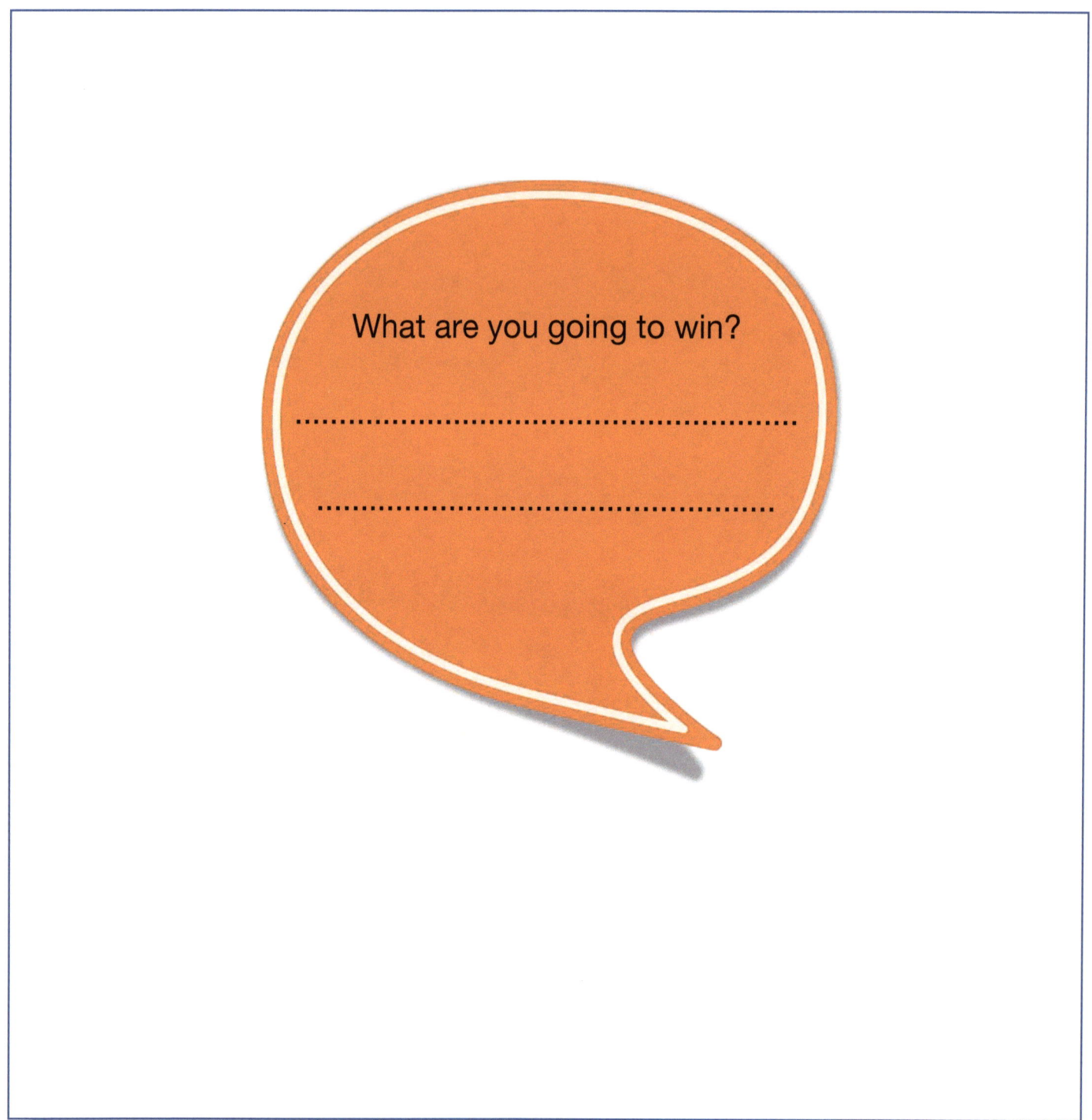

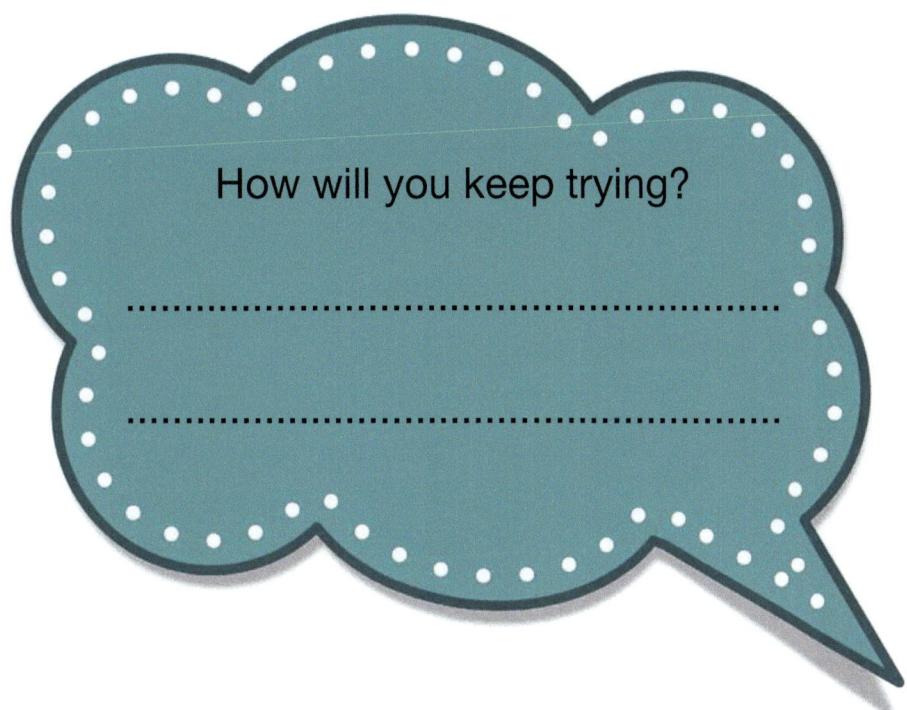

How will you keep trying?

....

....

And for his next achievement he wants to be in the
World Cup final. Find out about his journey and how
he improves his skills in the next book.

"Hi I'm Phoebe.
I like pasta with
chocolate and cheese and I like
playing football in midfield.
I hope you enjoy
this book."

"Hi I'm Isabel.
I like TV, football, ice cream
and running races."